DINOSAURS

Magic Matt and the Dinosaur
What the Dinosaurs Saw: Animals Living Then and Now
Dinosaur Garden
Dinosaurs

SCHOLASTIC INC. Cartwheel ·B·O·O·K·S·®

New York Toronto London Auckland Sydney
Mexico City New Delhi Hong Kong Buenos Aires

Magic Matt and the Dinosaur (ISBN 0-439-37607-6)
Text copyright © 2004 by Grace Maccarone.
Illustrations copyright © 2004 by Norman Bridwell.

What the Dinosaurs Saw: Animals Living Then and Now (ISBN 0-590-37128-2)
Text copyright © 1998 by Miriam Schlein.
Illustrations copyright © 1998 by Carol Schwartz.

Dinosaur Garden (ISBN 0-590-43172-2)
Copyright © 1990 by Liza Donnelly.

Dinosaurs (ISBN 0-439-20060-1)
Text copyright © 2001 by Grace Maccarone.
Illustrations copyright © 2001 by Richard Courtney.

All rights reserved. Published by Scholastic Inc.
SCHOLASTIC, CARTWHEEL BOOKS, and associated logos
are trademarks and/or registered trademarks of Scholastic Inc.

ISBN-13: 978-0-439-93251-6
ISBN-10: 0-439-93251-3

12 11   14 15 16/0
Printed in Singapore 46 • This compilation edition first printing, May 2007

TABLE OF CONTENTS

MAGIC MATT ™
and the Dinosaur

To Michelle
— G.M.

The author and illustrator thank Manny Campana for his contribution to this book.

MAGIC MATT ™
and the Dinosaur

by **Grace Maccarone**
Illustrated by **Norman Bridwell**

Hello! I am Magic Matt.
I can do magic.

See me make a turtle.
Zap!

No. That is a snake.
I want a turtle.
Zap!

No. That is a lizard.

I want a turtle.
Zap!

I made a dinosaur!
Cool!

Not so cool!
This dinosaur is a meat eater.

I will change it
to a plant eater.
Zap!

This is better.

27

Oh, no!
It eats our plants.
Mom will be mad.

30

Oh, no!
It breaks our chair.
Mom will be very,
very mad.

It runs out the door.
I run after it.

It chases a bus!

I must stop the dinosaur.
Zap!

Let's go home now, little turtle.

What the Dinosaurs Saw

ANIMALS LIVING THEN AND NOW

Mary and Harriete
— *C.S.*

The editors gratefully acknowledge the comments and advice
of Dr. E. H. Colbert of the Museum of Northern Arizona.

What the Dinosaurs Saw

ANIMALS LIVING THEN AND NOW

by **Miriam Schlein**

Illustrated by **Carol Schwartz**

Come with me.
We can see
things the dine
long ago.

We can see
a spider spinning,
same as the dinosaurs saw.

Two turtles resting
on a rock,
just as the dinosaurs saw.

We can see
three wiggly worms,
same as the dinosaurs saw.

Four little pine cones
falling from a tree
was something else
the dinosaurs could see.

Five frogs croaking.
The dinosaurs heard that, too,
long ago.

Six snakes sliding...

seven salamanders sleeping...

eight gulls gliding...

nine possums prowling...

All these things
the dinosaurs saw

are still here
for you and me to see.

The sun that warmed
the dinosaurs
still warms you.

And the same moon
that shines down on you
shined down long ago
on the dinosaurs, too.

DINOSAUR GARDEN

by **Liza Donnelly**

For Grace, Nina and Eden.

With special thanks to Dr. Paul Sereno, Assistant Professor, Department of Anatomy from the University of Chicago, for fact-checking the glossary.

"Bones! Let's plant a dinosaur garden.
It will be fun!"

"Some dinosaurs ate only plants."

"Things like fern and pine."

"First we buy seeds."

"We dig a hole."

"We drop in the seeds."

"Then we water."

81

"Yikes!"

"Where are we??"

"This looks like the time of the dinosaurs!"

"Bones, I think there are plant eaters here!"

*"We are *all* plant eaters!"

"Look, an egg."

"Is it yours?"   *"No!"

*"No!"   "Yours?"

"Is it yours?"   *"No!"

"Yours?"   *"No!"

*"Mama?"

"It's cute. It looks like…"

*"Run!!"

"Aaaah!! A baby Tyrannosaurus!!"   *"Mama!"

"… And it's a meat eater! Help!"

"Wow!"

"Thank you!"

"Look, Bones. Is that another egg?"

"Let's take it home."

"I wonder what kind of egg it is."

GLOSSARY

ANCHICERATOPS
(ANG-kee-sair-a-tops)

BRACHIOSAURUS
(BRAK-ee-uh-sawr-us)

HETERODONTOSAURUS
(het-er-uh-DON-tuh-sawr-us)

LEPTOCERATOPS
(lep-toe-SAIR-uh-tops)

MAIASAURA
(mah-ee-ah-SAWR-uh)

PARASAUROLOPHUS
(par-ah-sawr-OL-uh-fus)

POLACANTHUS
(po-luh-KANTH-us)

PTERODACTYLUS
(tair-uh-DAK-til-us)

TYRANNOSAURUS
(tye-RAN-uh-sawr-us)

PLANTS

EGG

DINOSAURS

DINOSAURS

by **Grace Maccarone**

Illustrated by **Richard Courtney**

Dinosaurs lived
long ago.

Fossils tell us
what we know.

Some were big.

Some were small.

Some were long.

Some were tall.

Some had beaks.

Some had sails.

Some had plates
and powerful tails.

Some had spikes

or bird-like feet.

Some ate plants.

And some ate meat.

Some had horns and bony frills.

Some had fancy crests and bills.

Some had sharp claws.

Some had strong jaws.

Some dinosaurs
fought each other.

Some of the young stayed
close to mother.

Some dinosaur eggs
hatched in a nest.

Which dinosaur do you like best?

Diplodocus

Ultrasaurus

Saltopus

Tyrannosaurus

Spinosaurus

Struthiomimus

Ankylosaurus

Stegosaurus

Iguanodon

Hypsilophodon

Dryosaurus

Allosaurus

Triceratops

Apatosaurus

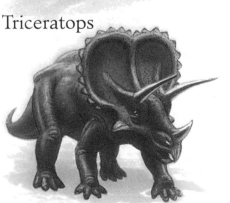

Deinonychus

Lambeosaurus

Protoceratops

Velociraptor

Homalocephale

Ceratosaurus

Maiasaura